Hannah Seeley is a full-time mom and an occupational therapist with passion and experience of working with young children. Hannah has a husband, two children (one girl and one boy), two crazy cats, and one goofy dog. When she's not writing books and playing with kids, Hannah loves to read, paint, and do fun crafts!

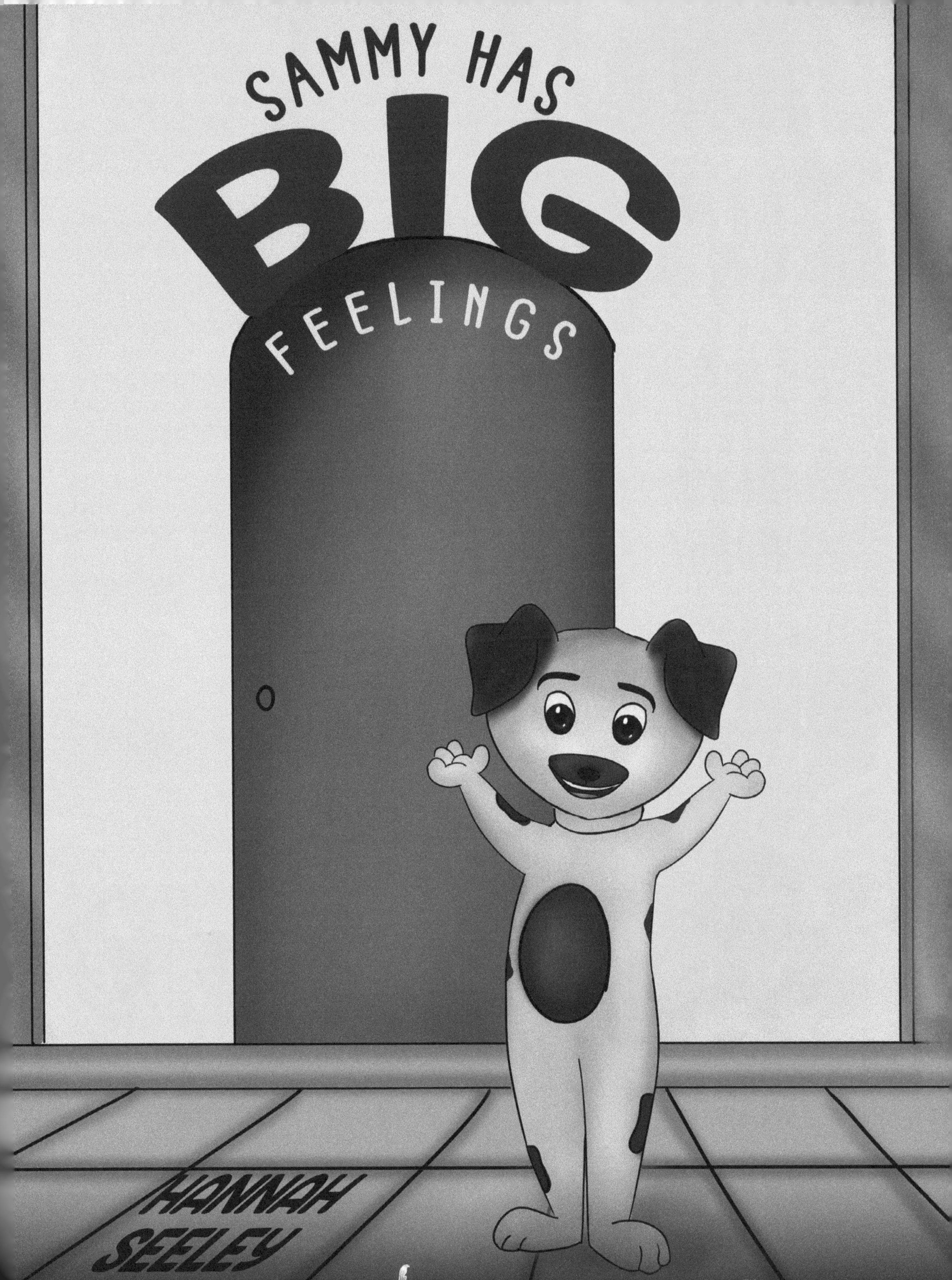

AUSTIN MACAULEY PUBLISHERS™

Copyright © Hannah Seeley 2021

Ordering Information
Quantity sales: Special discounts are available on quantity purchases by corporations, associations, and others. For details, contact the publisher at the address below.

Publisher's Cataloging-in-Publication data
Seeley, Hannah
Sammy Has Big Feelings

ISBN 9781649792624 (Paperback)
ISBN 9781649792631 (ePub e-book)

Library of Congress Control Number: 2021919376

www.austinmacauley.com/us

First Published 2021
Austin Macauley Publishers LLC
40 Wall Street 33rd Floor, Suite 3302
New York, NY 10005
USA

mail-usa@austinmacauley.com
+1 (646) 5125767

For my Sammy

This is **SAMMY.**

Sammy is a **HAPPY BO**

Sometimes, Sammy feels **SAD**, like when his mommy goes away.

She always comes back and Sammy has fun with Nanny, but he still feels sad.

Sometimes, Sammy feel mad,
like when he can't have his
FAVORITE SNACK.

Sammy always has
enough to eat, and
good things too, but
he still feels **MAD.**

Sometimes, Sammy feels **WORRIED**, like when he's in a new place and near new people.

Sammy wants to see and do new things, but still, Sammy feels **WORRIED**.

Sometimes, Sammy feels **TIRED** and he doesn't want to stop having fun.

Sammy has trouble controlling and saying how he feels, but Sammy feels tired.

Sometimes, Sammy feels **FRUSTRATED,** like when he feels big feelings and can't explain them or understand them.

It helps if a grown up is there, but Sammy feels **FRUSTRATED.**

Sometimes, Sammy needs a snack to help him feel **CALM** and **STRONG.**

12

Sometimes, Sammy needs to run and wiggle to help his body feel in **CONTROL** and **CALM.**

Sometimes, Sammy needs time alone to help him feel in **CONTROL AND CALM.**

Sometimes, Sammy needs to color any way he wants to help him feel **CALM AND SAFE.**

Sometimes, Sammy needs rest to help him feel **CALM** and **STRONG**.

Sometimes, Sammy needs to cuddle his blankie or stuffy to help him feel **SAFE** and **CALM**.

Sometimes, Sammy needs help to find something else to do so he can feel in **CONTROL** and **CALM**.

Sometimes, Sammy has
big feelings.

And **THAT IS OK.**

CPSIA information can be obtained
at www.ICGtesting.com
Printed in the USA
LVHW070433171121
703473LV00009B/498